# Contents

# Planet Earth

The Earth is the **planet** we live on. It is the third planet from the Sun. It is found between Mars and Venus.

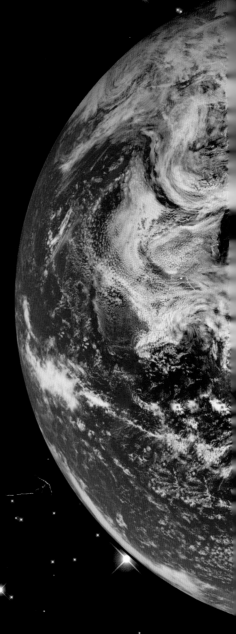

From space, the Earth looks like a blue, green and white marble.

5

# The Solar System

The **Solar System** is huge. There are eight planets in the Solar System. They all go around the Sun.

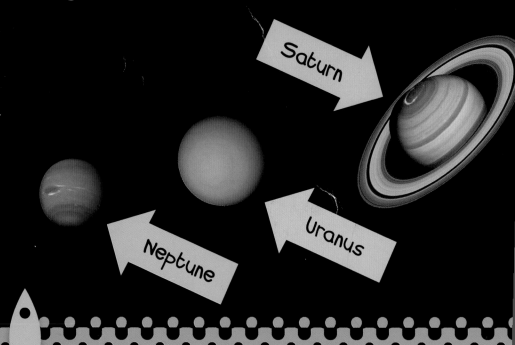

Saturn

Uranus

Neptune

Earth

Mercury

Venus

Sun

Mars

Jupiter

The Sun and the planets formed billions of years ago.

7

# Atmosphere

A thin layer of air surrounds the Earth. This is called the **atmosphere**. It keeps the planet safe.

atmosphere

The atmosphere keeps the Earth warm and lets plants, animals and people breathe.

# Inside the Earth

The Earth is made up of four layers. They are all different.

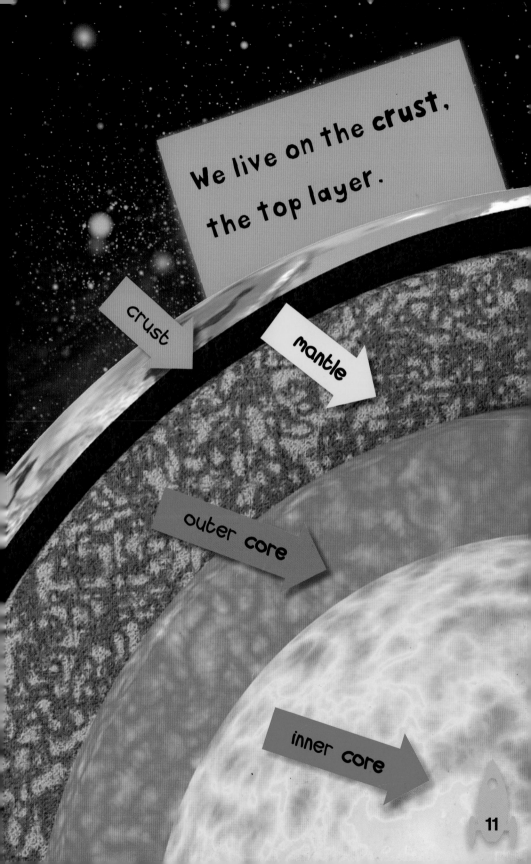

We live on the **crust**, the **top** layer.

crust

mantle

outer core

inner core

11

# Day and night

The Earth spins round. The Sun shines on one side of the Earth.

night-time

It is day on this side. It is night on the dark side.

# The seasons

It takes one year for the Earth to go around the Sun. The Earth is tilted.

spring

summer

Different parts of the Earth get more or less sunlight at different times of year. This is what makes the seasons.

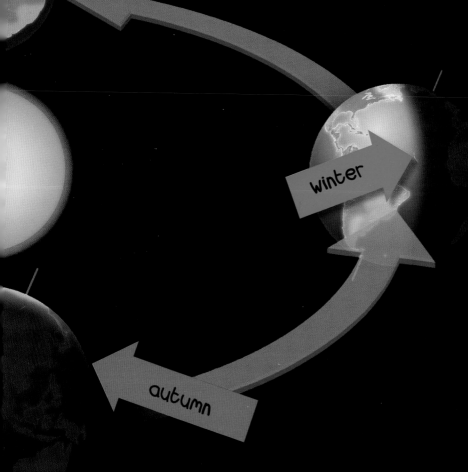

winter

autumn

# Mars

Mars is the fourth
planet from the sun.
It is found between
the Earth and Jupiter.
It is about half the
size of the Earth.

Earth

Mars

Jupiter

The planet looks red because it has red soil.

17

# The biggest volcano

Mars has a **volcano** called Olympus Mons. It is the biggest volcano in the Solar System.

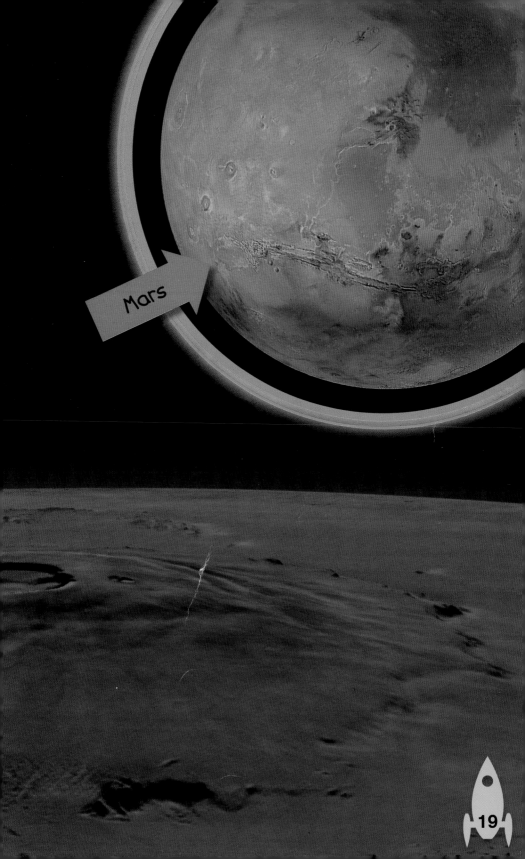

Mars

# Stormy planet

On Mars, there can be very fast winds. Sometimes the whole planet is one big dust storm.

dust storm

The red parts of
Mars are dust storms.
The dark parts
are rock.

# Rovers

Rovers are machines that work like robots. They are sent to explore Mars.

Scientists on Earth can drive rovers slowly over Mars.

camera

The rovers can go up hills and take photos.

# Glossary

**atmosphere** – the gases that surround a planet

**core** – the very hot inner part of the Earth

**crust** – the hard outer layer of the Earth

**dust storm** – strong winds carrying clouds of dust and dirt

**mantle** – the inner part of the Earth that is between the crust and the core

**planet** – one of the eight large objects circling the Sun

**rover** – a remote control vehicle for exploring another planet

**solar system** – the Sun and all of the things that move around it

**soil** – the top layer of dirt

**volcano** – a mountain through which melted rock, ash and hot gases can erupt